B

S0-ACU-668

WITHDRAWN

COPY 30

J398.2   Galdone, Paul.
CINDERELLA   Cinderella / Paul Galdone. -- New
             York : McGraw-Hill, c1978.   bk1 PS-2
             [40] p. : col. ill.

                SUMMARY: A mistreated kitchen maid,
             with the help of her fairy godmother,
             attends the palace ball on the condi-
             tion that she leave before midnight.
                ISBN 0-07-022684-9 : 10.95 lib.

             1.Fairy tales. 2.Folklore--France.

Livonia Public Library   70200   My84
CARL SANDBURG BRANCH
50100 W. 7 Mile Road   78-7614
Livonia, Mich. 48152   MARC

WITHDRAWN [1]

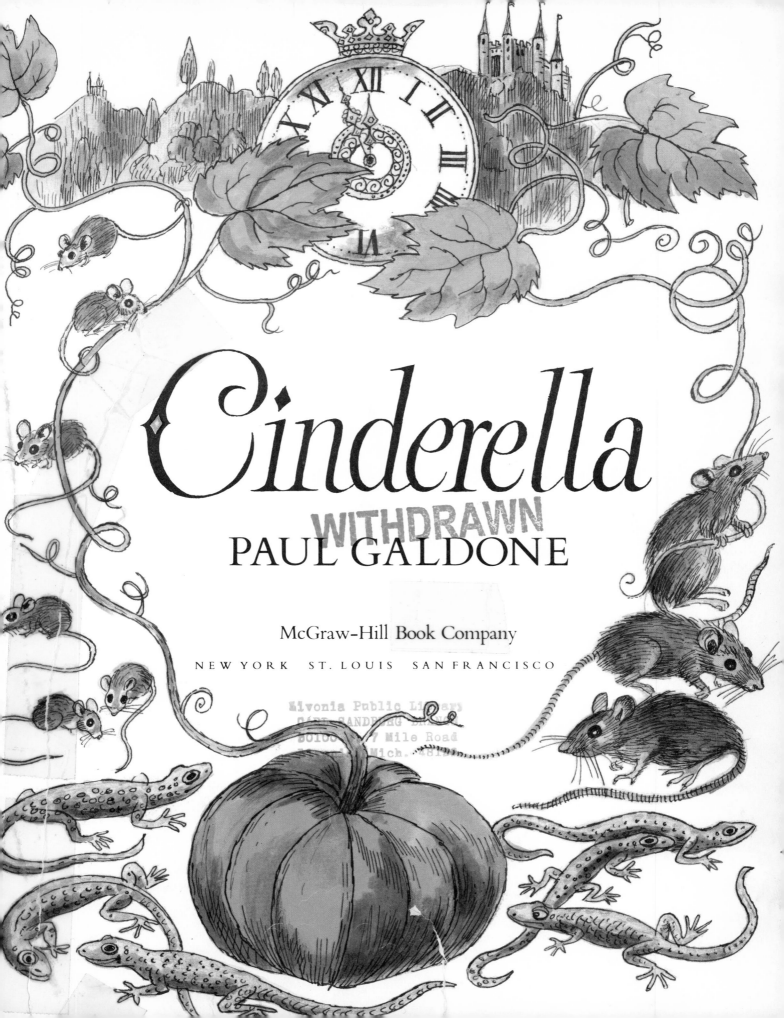

Cinderella

PAUL GALDONE

WITHDRAWN

McGraw-Hill Book Company

NEW YORK   ST. LOUIS   SAN FRANCISCO

Livonia Public Library
CARL SANDBURG BRANCH
30100   7 Mile Road
           Mich. 48154

For Thordis

3 9082 04827317 4

Library of Congress Cataloging in Publication Data
Galdone, Paul.   Cinderella.
Summary: A mistreated kitchen maid, with the help
of her fairy godmother, attends the palace ball on the
condition that she leave before midnight.
[1. Fairy tales. 2. Folklore—France.] I. Title.
PZ8.G127Ci   [398.2] [E]   78-7614
ISBN 0-07-022684-9

Copyright © 1978 by Paul Galdone. All Rights Reserved. Printed in the United States of America. No part
of this publication may be reproduced, stored in a retrieval system, or transmitted, in any form or by any
means, electronic, mechanical, photocopying, recording, or otherwise, without the prior written permission of
the publisher.

2 3 4 5 6 7 8 9   R A B P   7 8 3 2 1 0 9

C30

Once there lived a nobleman who, after his first wife died, took for his second wife the haughtiest and proudest woman in the land. She had two daughters who were just like her. The nobleman himself had a daughter, who was sweet and kind as her own mother had been.

The wedding was hardly over when the stepmother became jealous of her husband's daughter, for the young girl's goodness made her daughters seem even more unpleasant. The stepmother commanded the girl to sweep and scrub the floors, scour the pots, and wait on herself and her two daughters from early morning till night.

The girl slept up in the attic on a lumpy straw mat while her stepsisters had fine rooms with inlaid floors, soft beds, and tall mirrors in which they could admire themselves from head to foot.

She suffered all patiently, not daring to complain to her father, for his new wife ruled him completely. When her daily work was done, she would sit down in the chimney-corner among the ashes, and so her sisters gave her the nickname Cinderella.

But Cinderella in her shabby clothes was far more beautiful than her stepsisters, richly dressed as they were.

It happened that year the King's son gave a ball and invited all the notables from far and near. The two stepsisters were invited among others. They were delighted and soon they were busy choosing the gowns, petticoats and headdresses that would be most becoming.

This meant more work for Cinderella, for it was she who ironed their linens and hemmed their skirts. They did nothing but talk of their clothes and gaze into their mirrors.

"I," said the elder, "shall wear my red velvet gown and my collar of English lace."

"And I," said the younger, "shall have only my plain evening dress, but to make up for it, I shall wear a cloak embroidered with golden flowers and my diamond clasp, which is not to be ridiculed."

They were so excited that they did not eat for almost two days. They broke more than a dozen laces trying to tighten their corsets so they would look slim.

At last the great day arrived. Hairdressers were sent for to arrange the stepsisters' hair in the most fashionable styles. Ribbons and beauty patches were brought from the best shops. The stepsisters called Cinderella for advice, for she had excellent ideas, and they welcomed her help in making them look their best.

While she waited on them they asked, "Cinderella, would you not like to go to the ball?"

"Oh, you are making fun of me," she replied. "It is not a place for such as I."

"You are right," they said. "People would laugh to see a cinder-maid at the ball!"

Anyone but Cinderella would have tangled their hair for them. But she had a sweet nature and saw that they were dressed perfectly.

That evening they set out for the ball. Cinderella watched them until they were out of sight. Then she could hold back her tears no longer. She began to cry.

Suddenly her godmother appeared. "What is the matter, child?" she asked. "I wish... I wish I could..." was all Cinderella could say through her sobs.

"You wish you could go to the ball, isn't that so?"
"Yes," Cinderella agreed and sighed sadly.

"Well," said the godmother, who was a fairy, "just be a good girl, and I will see that you go. First," she said, "run into the garden and bring me a pumpkin."

Cinderella hurried to find the roundest pumpkin there was. She brought it to her godmother who hollowed it out and struck it with her wand. Instantly, it turned into a fine golden coach.

Then her godmother looked into the mousetrap, where she found six live mice. She asked Cinderella to lift the door, and, as each mouse scurried out, she tapped it gently with her wand.

At once each mouse became a fine horse.
Altogether they made an elegant set of six dapple-gray horses.

"Now I must find something to change into a coachman," said the godmother.

"I will go and see if there is a rat in the rat trap," said Cinderella. "We could make a coachman out of him."

"Go and look," replied the godmother.

Cinderella brought the trap to her and in it were three huge rats. The godmother chose the one with the longest whiskers, and when she touched it with her wand it became a fat, jolly coachman who had the smartest mustache ever to be seen.

"Now," she said to Cinderella, "go again to the garden, child, and you will find six lizards behind the watering pot. Bring them to me."

As soon as Cinderella had done so, her godmother turned them into six footmen. They were dressed in gleaming livery, and they stood in position around the coach as if they had been doing nothing else all their lives.

The godmother then said to Cinderella: "Well, here you have a coach fit to carry you to the ball. Aren't you pleased?"

"Oh, yes!" cried Cinderella. "But can I go there as I am in these nasty rags?"

Her godmother didn't answer. Instead, she waved her wand over Cinderella, and the tattered clothes were turned into cloth of gold and silver set with sparkling precious stones. Then her godmother gave her a pair of glass slippers, the prettiest in all the world.

As Cinderella stepped up into the coach, her godmother warned, "Do not stay till after midnight, for if you stay one moment longer, the coach will once again be a pumpkin; the horses, mice; the footmen, lizards; the coachman a rat; and your clothes will become rags as before."

Cinderella shuddered. "I promise, dear godmother, that I will surely leave the ball before midnight." And so she set out for the palace, bursting with joy.

The King's son, when he was told that a great princess whom nobody knew had arrived, hurried to greet her. He helped her alight from the coach and led her into the great hall where the company had gathered. There was a sudden hush. The dancing stopped, the violinists and other musicians ceased to play, and a murmur arose: "How beautiful she is! How beautiful she is!"

The King himself, as old as he was, could not help watching her. He whispered to the Queen that it had been a long time since he had seen so lovely a creature. The men were fascinated by her beauty. The ladies busily studied her clothes and headdress so that they could have some made like them the next day; that is, if they could find such fine materials and skilled hands to fashion them.

The King's son seated Cinderella in a place of honor and afterward led her out to dance with him. She danced so gracefully that she was admired more and more. Later a fine supper was served, but the Prince was so absorbed in gazing at Cinderella that he did not eat a bite.

She went and sat down by her sisters. She spoke pleasantly with them and to their surprise graciously shared with them some of the oranges and other fruit the Prince had given her. They did not recognize their shabby stepsister. While Cinderella was visiting her sisters, she heard the clock strike a quarter to twelve. Immediately she made a deep courtsey to the company and hurried away as fast as she could.

When she got home, Cinderella found her fairy godmother was still there. She thanked her and told her the King's son had begged her to come again the following night to another ball.

Before her godmother could say anything, her two stepsisters knocked loudly on the door and Cinderella ran to open it. "How long you have stayed!" she said, yawning and stretching and rubbing her eyes as if she had just awakened.

"If you had been at the ball," said one of the sisters, "you would not have felt sleepy. A beautiful princess came there, one of the loveliest ever seen! She was polite and friendly to us and even gave us oranges and citrons."

Cinderella was secretly delighted. She asked the name of the princess but they answered, "It is a mystery! No one knows! The King's son would give anything to know who she is."

At this, Cinderella smiled and said, "She must then have been very beautiful, indeed. How fortunate you have been. If only I could see her!" She asked her older sister, "Oh please, couldn't you lend me your yellow gown that you wear for every day?"

"Well, really!" cried her haughty stepsister, "lend my clothes to a dirty cinder-grub like you! I'd be a fool." Of course, Cinderella had expected such an answer and was relieved by the refusal.

The next day the two sisters were again at the ball. So was Cinderella, this time dressed even more splendidly than before. The King's son stayed by her side, saying kind and flattering things to her. His words so pleased her that she forgot all about her godmother's warning.

Suddenly, she heard the clock striking midnight.

In panic, she fled from the ballroom as lightly as a deer. The Prince followed her, but she disappeared before he could overtake her. All there was left was one of her little glass slippers which he picked up tenderly. The guards at the palace gates were asked if they had seen the princess go out, but they said they had seen no one but a young girl in ragged work clothes.

Cinderella arrived home quite out of breath, and in her nasty old clothes. Nothing at all of her finery was left but the mate of the slipper she had lost.

When the two sisters returned from the ball, Cinderella asked them if they had enjoyed themselves and if the fine lady had been there. They told her she had been present, but suddenly, at the stroke of midnight, she had fled in such haste that she had dropped one of her little glass slippers, the prettiest in the world.

The Prince had picked it up. All the rest of the night, he sat gazing at the slipper.

"He must be deeply in love with the beautiful princess," said the younger stepsister, who was the kinder of the two.

What she said was true, for a few days later the King's herald read a proclamation to the sound of trumpets that the King's son would marry the one whose foot the slipper would just fit.

The Prince's messengers went about trying the slipper on all the princesses, then the duchesses and all the women of the court, but in vain. Several days later it was brought to the two sisters. Each one tried her best to force her foot into the slipper, but neither one could. Cinderella, who was watching and knew that it was her slipper, laughed and said,

"Why not let me see if it will fit me?" The sisters sneered and made fun of her, but the King's messenger said it was only fair, for he had been ordered to try the slipper on every young girl. He asked her to sit down, and on putting the slipper on her small foot, he saw that it fitted as snugly as if it had been made of wax. Then to the amazement of the two sisters, Cinderella drew the other slipper from her pocket and put it on her other foot.

Suddenly the godmother appeared in the room, and when she touched Cinderella's clothes with her wand, they became even more magnificent than those she had worn to the ball.

The two sisters now knew Cinderella was the lovely princess they had seen at the ball. They threw themselves at her feet and begged her pardon for treating her so badly. Cinderella helped them to stand up, and as she hugged them she said she loved them with all her heart and asked them always to love her.

The beautiful Cinderella was taken to the young Prince. He found her more charming than ever and a few days later they were married. Cinderella, who was as good as she was beautiful, brought her two stepsisters to live at the palace and soon married them to two great lords of the court.